rah
&
uck

ay at

THE DUCK HOTEL

Sarah and Duck arrive at the hotel.
A **very** fancy hotel, indeed.

Oh look – other ducks are staying here too!

says the receptionist.

Nest?

Nest?
Did he really say 'nest'?

That's right, madam.

The receptionist gives Sarah and Duck a key to their room.

Enjoy your stay!

Oh, you might want to put on your swimming costume . . .

says the receptionist.

It looks like it could get quite splashy around here!

Sarah and Duck head up to find their room.

Oh yes! This is very nice.

Sarah unpacks her swimming costume and puts it on.

Meanwhile, Duck gets
comfortable in his nest.

Umm. Where's
my bed?

Well, Sarah, this
is a duck hotel!

No matter how hard she tries to nest, Sarah cannot get comfortable!

I know – why don't we do some exploring?

Yes! Let's find the pool!

says Sarah.

Wow! A hotel helter-skelter. I wonder if it leads to the pool?

Sarah comes whizzing down the slide and crashes . . . straight into Duck's bottom.

Are you all right, Sarah?

Well, it looks like you've found the pool. There are lots of ducks here.

But which one is **our** duck?

Phew! You found him. How about we go and dry off?

Time for a spot of preening.
It certainly looks like Duck's settling in!

Sarah waits for her feather preen but it doesn't come.
Maybe you need a few more feathers, Sarah?

Come on, some tasty dinner will cheer you up . . .

Hmm. What's for starters?

Quack!

Ah, bread! Your favourite, Duck.

Wow, more bread!
Aren't you a lucky duck!

Oh look!
Another course, and it's . . .

After dinner, Duck sits with the other ducks for a chat.
Sarah tries to quack along with the conversation . . .

Qu . . . aaa . . . cck!?

. . . but they don't
really understand her.

Oh! Sarah sighs.

Still feeling a bit left out, eh, Sarah?

Uh huh.

Oh look, here's Duck . . . and I
think he wants you to go with him.

Where are we
going, Duck?

asks Sarah.

Ooooo!

Then all the ducks shuffle Sarah towards the middle of a big glass room.

Duck pushes a **big** red button and a huge fan begins to whirl. The ducks start to drift up into the air.

Well, I never! You're floating, Sarah!

The End